WILLIAM'S GETAWAY

WRITTEN BY Annika Dunklee   ILLUSTRATED BY Yong Ling Kang

OWLKIDS BOOKS

William has a little brother.
His name is Edgar.

Edgar loves to play with William.

And sometimes...

Sometimes William likes to play with Edgar.

But today . . .

Today William has had
enough of Edgar.

"You wanna build a fort, William?"

"No."

"You wanna play monster truck smash-up, William?"

"No."

"You wanna smash up bananas, William ... with monster trucks?"

"No!?"

"You wanna—"

William wanted some time by himself.
All by himself.

And the only place for William to get that was …

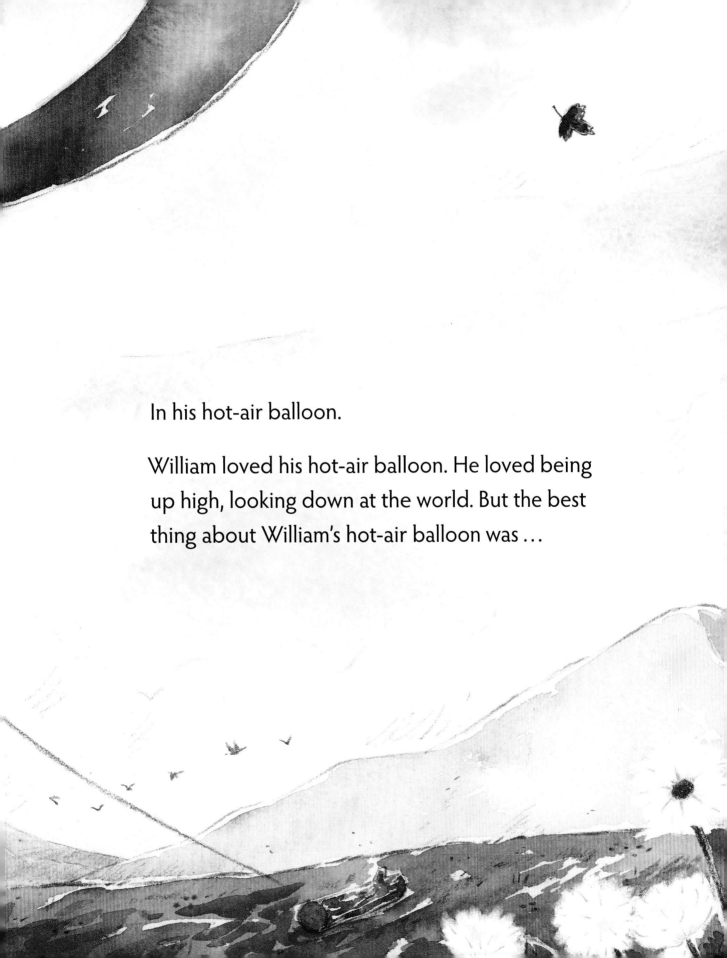

In his hot-air balloon.

William loved his hot-air balloon. He loved being up high, looking down at the world. But the best thing about William's hot-air balloon was …

Edgar wouldn't go up in it.
He was too scared.

But on this day ...

"Hold on, William! Wait for me!"

William was very surprised and extremely disappointed.

"But, Edgar, I thought you were too scared."

"I was. But Mom says I'll be okay—I'll be with YOU!"

William sighed.

But then . . .

"Wait! What if I
get hungry, William?"

"And what if I
get thirsty?"

"I'm *all* ready,"
said Edgar.

"HANG ON!"

"What if I get cold, William?"

"Or what if I get bored?"

Swish!
Whirr!

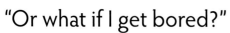

Edgar was finally about to start up the ladder when …

"What if … what if … I get scared, William?"

"I NEED MR. BIBBLES!!"

Edgar tucked Mr. Bibbles under his chin
and started slowly picking up his things.

"EDGAR, STOP!

You don't
need
anything."

"Not even Mr. Bibbles?"

"Not even Mr. Bibbles."

Edgar put everything down. Even Mr. Bibbles.

"Don't worry, little guy. I'll be okay—I'll be with William."

Edgar put his foot on the first step of the ladder.
Then stopped.

"You've got this," said William.

Edgar climbed onto the second step.
And stopped again.

"I can't do it, William. I just can't!"

"Yes, you can."

Edgar looked at William, who was
holding out his hand. He took a deep
breath and continued his climb.

"I've got you!" said William, pulling Edgar
up and into the hot-air balloon.

"William! I did it!" exclaimed Edgar.

Edgar loves to play with William. And sometimes, sometimes William likes to play with Edgar. But not today...

Today William *loves* playing with Edgar.

*To Suzanne, for taking
the top bunk* —A.D.

―――――――

*For Alexander and
Theodore* —Y.L.K.

Text © 2020 Annika Dunkee | Illustrations © 2020 Yong Ling Kang

Owlkids Books acknowledges the financial support of the Canada Council for the Arts, the Ontario Arts Council, the Government of Canada through the Canada Book Fund (CBF) and the Government of Ontario through the Ontario Creates Book Initiative for our publishing activities.

Published in Canada by
Owlkids Books Inc.
1 Eglinton Avenue East
Toronto, ON M4P 3A1

Published in the United States by
Owlkids Books Inc.
1700 Fourth Street
Berkeley, CA 94710

Library of Congress Control Number: 2019947229

Library and Archives Canada Cataloguing in Publication

Title: William's getaway / written by Annika Dunklee ; illustrated by Yong Ling Kang.
Names: Dunklee, Annika, 1965- author. | Kang, Yong Ling illustrator.
Identifiers: Canadiana 20190115602 | ISBN 9781771473378 (hardcover)
Classification: LCC PS8607.U542 W55 2020

Edited by Debbie Rogosin | Designed by Alisa Baldwin

Manufactured in Shenzhen, Guangdong, China,
in October 2019, by C&C Offset
Job #HT5021

A   B   C   D   E   F

Publisher of Chirp, Chickadee and OWL
www.owlkidsbooks.com

Owlkids Books is a division of bayard canada